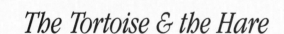

The Tortoise & the Hare

An Aesop Fable

Adapted by:
Ken Forsse
Margaret Ann Hughes

Illustrated by:
Russell Hicks
Douglas McCarthy
Theresa Mazurek
Allyn Conley-Gorniak
Julie Ann Armstrong

This Book Belongs To:

Use this symbol to match book and cassette.

nce upon a time there lived a tortoise…which is another name for a turtle. The tortoise was named Leonard.

Now a tortoise is by nature very slow, and Leonard was no exception. He took forever to do anything.

He was late wherever he went. He was always late for dinner, and he was always the last one to go to bed at night.

Now everyone understood that it was alright for Leonard to be slow because he was a tortoise…everyone but the hare, that is.

Now a hare is a kind of rabbit…and very fast.

Well, the hare was named Skip, and he was always picking on Leonard.

Skip wouldn't stop teasing Leonard. He didn't seem to realize that animals are not all the same.

Well, Skip kept making Leonard feel bad about being slow, until finally, the tortoise had enough of the hare's teasing.

Oh my, Leonard made a very bold statement. He challenged Skip to a race…a foot race! It seemed rather foolish. How could a tortoise beat a hare in a race?

Well, all of the rest of the forest animals became very interested.

It was decided that the race would be in one week, on Saturday, at 12 o'clock sharp. Leonard and Skip would race from the oak tree in the meadow, down the road, around the big rock by the stream, past

the clover patch, over the hill and back to the oak tree.

During the week, Skip spent his time telling everyone he met how he was going to beat the slow tortoise.

While the hare was bragging, the tortoise was
practicing for the race with the help of Pamela,
a tiny bird.

With Pam's encouraging, Leonard went over every
inch of the race again and again.

Oh, the tortoise worked very, very hard. He was
determined to win the race. Finally, it was Saturday.

Everyone in the forest was gathered by the oak tree to watch this unusual race.

Leonard was even early.

Skip was almost late for the start of the race because he had been so busy bragging about how he was going to win.

Well, it was finally 12 o'clock. Leonard and Skip lined up at the starting line.

My goodness! Skip rushed off like a shot. He actually did leave Leonard in a cloud of dust.

Leonard trudged along as fast as he could, but Skip ran so fast that he was soon out of sight.

The tortoise kept moving at a slow, but steady, pace. It wasn't long, though, before the hare had reached the big rock by the stream and headed back past the clover patch.

Well, the sun was a little warm that day, and the hare was sure that he would win the race. So he sat down for a moment in the nice cool clover.

Leonard kept going at a steady pace. Because of all his practicing, he knew how to run the race, and he wasn't getting tired. Meanwhile, the clover was so cool and felt so good, that Skip decided to lie down for a little while. It wouldn't matter. He would easily win the race anyway. But Leonard kept moving along all the way down the road, around past the rock, by the stream, and then past the clover patch.

Well sure enough, the hare had fallen asleep in the clover. The tortoise quietly tiptoed by him and headed over the hill and toward the oak tree.

All of the animals at the oak tree were wondering why Skip was not back yet. When they saw Leonard coming over the hill, they were very surprised and excited. They started cheering!

Well, all of the noise and excitement woke Skip up.

As Skip started over the hill, he looked down and saw Leonard getting close to the finish line.

Skip started running as fast as he could toward the oak tree and the finish line.

Everyone started yelling! No one could tell who was going to win. Leonard got closer to the finish line, and Skip was running faster and faster.

Then, just before Skip passed him, Leonard's nose crossed the finish line, and…

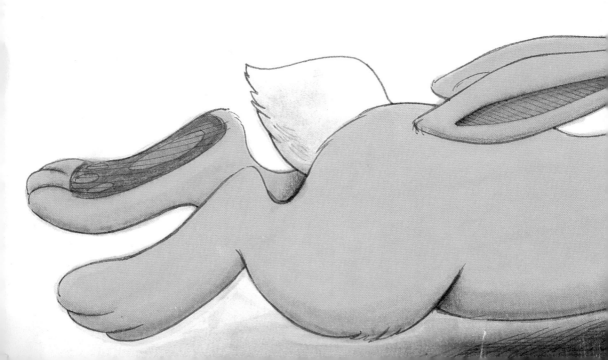

...yes indeed, Leonard the tortoise
had won the race. Skip was
very upset, as everyone
congratulated Leonard.

Well, eventually, even Skip understood that it was his own fault that he had lost the race, and he apologized to Leonard.

And so, both the tortoise and the hare learned a valuable lesson. It doesn't really matter how slow or how fast you are at doing things. The main thing is that you always do your very best.

nd they all lived happily ever after.